THE
A C
B

with

HONORA LEE

For my sisters, Clare and Margaret Mary;
and for all the other wondrous caregivers in the Loop.

Thank you, Eva, for poetic intervention.

THE
A C
B

with
HONORA LEE

by KATE DE GOLDI
drawings by GREGORY O'BRIEN

TUNDRA BOOKS

Text copyright © 2012 Kate De Goldi
Illustrations copyright © 2012 Gregory O'Brien

Published by arrangement with Random House New Zealand Ltd.
Published in North America by Tundra Books, 2014

Published in Canada by Tundra Books,
a division of Random House of Canada Limited,
One Toronto Street, Suite 300, Toronto, Ontario M5C 2V6

Published in the United States by Tundra Books of Northern New York,
P.O. Box 1030, Plattsburgh, New York 12901

Library of Congress Control Number: 2013943839

Library and Archives Canada Cataloguing in Publication

De Goldi, Kate, 1959-, author
The ACB with Honora Lee / written and illustrated by
Kate De Goldi.

Issued in print and electronic formats.
ISBN 978-1-77049-722-1 (bound).—ISBN 978-1-77049-723-8
(epub)

I. Title.

PZ7.D357Ab 2013   j823'.92   C2013-904468-X

Cover design: Megan van Staden
Cover drawing: Gregory O'Brien
The artwork in this book was rendered in ink and acrylic on paper.
This book is set in Mrs. Eaves

www.tundrabooks.com

Printed and bound in China

1 2 3 4 5 6   19 18 17 16 15 14

Poem

Three nots like
Three nots like

How do you what?
How do you what?

Claude

before

little beasts

That summer there seemed to be a lot of bumblebees around. Perry's father complained about it a
good deal. They were all over the footpaths, he
said, half asleep, or half dead. He kept almost
standing on them. It was extremely hazardous, he
said. For him and the bumblebees.

'What's wrong with the little beasts?' he said to

Perry's mother. 'Why aren't they buzzing about pollinating? Isn't that their job?'

He was cross and sweaty, Perry's father. He'd walked all the way home from work because it was good for him, but his bag had been heavy with papers, which was not at all good for him, it made his arm sore. And he'd had to dodge dozens of bumblebees.

'I don't know what's wrong with them,' said Perry's mother. 'I'm not a zoologist.'

She was a psychologist.

'Maybe they're hot,' she said. 'Or tired. Like you.'

'Bet it's global warming,' said Perry's father, gloomily. 'Or insecticides. Or polluted water. Or something we don't even know about yet.'

He often said things like this.

'It's probably not,' said Perry's mother.

'Maybe bumblebees are just getting stupider,' said Perry. She was thinking of becoming a zoologist when she grew up.

'There's no such word as stupider,' said both her parents together.

Perry looked up from the picture she was drawing. (It was a spider making a web.)

'There is now,' she said.

Perry was the only child in her family. She went to the Ernle Clark School because her parents said that was the best place for someone like her.

What was someone like her *like*? Perry often wondered. But she said, 'Why? Why? Why? Why is it the best school?'

'Because,' said her mother. 'Be . . . Cos . . .' She was driving the car, she couldn't think at the same time. She had to wait for the lights to turn red. 'Because it asks a lot of you.'

Actually, at school, it was Perry who asked a lot, though some of the teachers wished she would not. The Special Assistance teacher, Mrs. Sonne, said it would be better for everyone if Perry tried much harder to *listen.*

Perry's mother believed only children must be kept busy. They needed plenty of activities, she said, they needed to have plenty of other people in their life.

'How about a dog?' said Perry. But dogs were rackety and messy, said her mother, they left dog hair everywhere. People got allergies.

'What people?' said Perry. 'What allergies?'

'*Which* allergies,' said her mother, not really answering.

So there was no dog. There was no cat either, not a canary, a mouse, or a tortoise, which were some

9

of the other animals Perry had suggested. There was just Perry and her parents, and week after week after week full to the brim with after-school activities and other people.

Monday was piano with Gabriel. Gabriel had a nose stud and hair in a high ponytail and a cracked laugh. She was very patient with Perry who found it almost impossible to read the music *and* count *and* make her hands do different things at more or less the same time. Perry was still on the *Faber Piano Adventures Gold Star Performance Primer Level* after two whole years.

Never mind, said Gabriel, giving her cracked, hiccoughy laugh when Perry banged her head on the music rack in frustration. She patted Perry's back comfortingly. Slow and steady was just the way for some people, she said.

'And tortoises,' said Perry.

Wednesday was clarinet class with James who went to university and taught music in his spare time. James had a bass clef tattoo on his left wrist and a treble clef on his right.

There were three other students in the clarinet class and they made sweet and soaring sounds on their instruments. Much sweeter than Perry's sounds which mostly came out barking or burpy. James had never actually said this, but Perry just

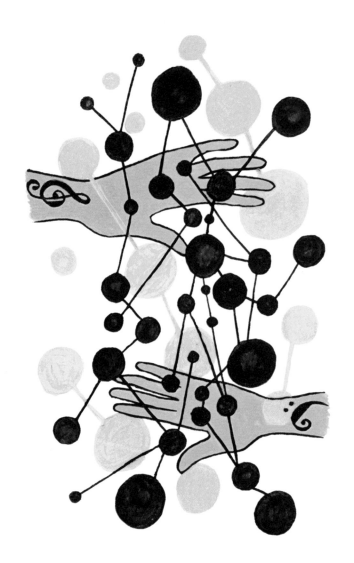

knew it. The other students looked down at the floor or up at the ceiling or out the window when she played *Go tell Aunt Rhody* or *Funeral March* by Frédéric Chopin, which were her two main tunes.

On Tuesdays Perry had After School Tutoring at the Thorrington Community Center with Haruka Homework. Her real name was Haruka Holme, but Perry silently called her Haruka Homework because tutoring lessons were long and exhausting, much like homework, though Haruka was very pretty and just as patient as Gabriel. She was kind, too. When Perry did particularly well with her writing or her maths Haruka gave her an origami animal fashioned from washi paper which was delicate and beautifully patterned. So far, Perry had a swan, a tiger and a frog. She was aiming for a whole zoo, but the going was slow.

On Thursdays Perry went again to the Community Center, for Music and Movement Class. M'n'M was directed by Brita, who was small and black-eyed and gave instructions too rapidly, so that Perry found it hard to keep up. Brita shouted at Perry to *concentrate*. She said Perry had the most eccentric sense of rhythm she'd ever come across.

'What does eccentric mean?' Perry asked her mother.

'Unconventional,' said her mother.

Perry's mother was sitting on the green sofa at the time, embroidering a matching moss green and russet cushion cover. She had been doing it for almost a hundred years. Her mother could only give very short answers when she was embroidering, and only occasionally, so Perry went to her bedroom and drew a picture of Brita.

She wrote BRITA in block letters beneath the picture in case someone mistook it for a boa constrictor or the eye of a cyclone. After a while she came back and sat on the tawny brown sofa watching her mother's needle move in and out, in and out, though embroidery certainly wasn't much of a spectator sport.

'What is it?' said her mother.

'What does unconventional mean?'

'Different from the usual.'

'Usual what?'

'Other people's usual.'

'So, is it a good thing?'

'It depends.'

'On what?'

'Good question,' said her mother, snipping the yarn with an efficient click of her embroidery scissors. She looked up at Perry and grimaced.

'You've been sucking again. There's felt pen all around your mouth. Go and get a face cloth.'

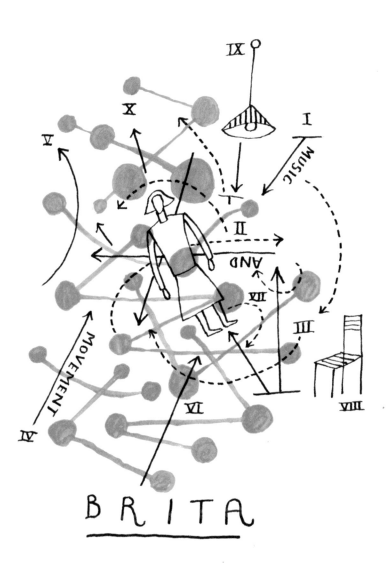

IX

X

V

I

MUSIC

II

AND

VII

III

MOVEMENT

IV

VI

VIII

BRITA

Conversations with her mother often went like this.

But Fridays were the best because there was Nina who had been Perry's nanny since she was very small. Nina came all the other weekdays too, but on Fridays Perry could go straight home to Nina and Claude and a plate of Nina's just-baked Belgian Biscuits.

Claude was Nina's little boy; he was two-nearly-three and came with Nina every afternoon. On Fridays, while Nina folded washing and put away dishes and prepared dinner, Claude followed Perry all around the house. He liked everything Perry did but he especially enjoyed her making violent hunting noises on the clarinet or playing Black Magic on the piano.

Black Magic was Perry's best piece. She had composed it herself. It was all the black notes on the piano played very fast and loud and in clumps, up and down, up and down, over and over again in whatever rhythm she felt like.

Black Magic was Perry's parents' least favorite piece, so she only gave recitals of it to Claude and Nina and her small origami zoo.

he's your Sunley

On Saturdays Perry and her father visited Perry's grandmother, who lived at Santa Lucia in the loop

of the river. Until that summer Perry had seen
Gran only once before, when she was two years old,
though she didn't remember this. Gran had lived
near Uncle Oscar and his wife, but Uncle Oscar
had gone to Istanbul on a whim and now it was
Perry's father's turn.

So far, all Perry knew about Gran was her name
— Honora Lee — and her age — seventy-six years
old — and that she didn't have a husband or much
memory any more, which was why she lived at Santa
Lucia and could never get Perry's father's name

right. Also, that she once had three brothers but they were all dead now. They were *deceased*, said Perry's father. The brothers had been called Bosco, Vincent and Hughie. These were the names Gran usually called Perry's father, though his name was actually Jonathan.

Perry and her father visited Gran for forty minutes, which Perry's father said was quite long enough. They sat in the small living room where there was a view of a garden fence covered in vines. Perry sat, like Gran, against the large peacock cushions and stared out the window at the vines, green and luscious. Perry's father asked Gran a lot of questions that she mostly didn't answer.

If Perry's father left the room Gran asked Perry questions instead.

'Who is that man?' said Gran.

'He's my dad,' said Perry. 'His name is Jonathan Sunley. He's your son.'

He's your Sunley, thought Perry, smiling, but she didn't say that to Gran in case it was confusing.

'Are you Imogen?' said Gran.

'No,' said Perry. 'I'm Perry.'

'That's a boy's name.' Gran squinted at Perry. 'Are you a boy? Where *is* Imogen?'

'I don't know. And, I'm a girl.'

'Your hair's short.'

'So is yours.' This wasn't rude because it was true. Gran's hair was short and thin and close to her head, like a swimming cap.

'She's probably late,' said Gran. 'She'll be late for her own funeral.'

'Probably,' said Perry. She couldn't think what else to say.

'I spy with my little eye,' said Gran.

'Goody,' said Perry. She liked I Spy.

'Something beginning with spectacles,' said Gran. She pointed her bent finger at Perry's spectacles, which were hard to miss.

'You're supposed to say a *letter*,' said Perry. 'You should say, "I spy with my little eye, something beginning with S."'

'Well, best be going,' said Gran. 'No rest for the wicked.'

And she stood up and walked away, which was usually how a visit to Gran ended.

forgotten

That was how it was with Gran. She seemed always to be walking away; she was off to tidy something up, or organize some people, or look for her pupils.

'Where *are* her pupils?' Perry asked.

'There aren't any pupils,' said her mother.

'Why is she looking for them then?'

'It's her memory. It's gone. She's forgotten she's retired and the pupils don't come any more.'

'What did they come for?'

'This and that. Extra lessons. Literacy, music, speech and drama—'

'A *school*teacher,' said Perry. This was a most disappointing piece of news.

'Not exactly,' said her mother. 'She didn't teach

at schools. She was alternative. Different.'

'Different than what?'

'Different *from*.'

'Well *what*?' said Perry.

'Different from everyone else.'

'Oh,' said Perry, pleased. 'Unconventional.'

moles are excellent tunnelers

On Sundays Perry and her mother and father went out for brunch at The Café on the Hill. This was for Family Time.

Family Time would be quite a lot better, Perry thought, if there were more family, some cousins, or aunts, perhaps. But there were no cousins and no aunts except Uncle Oscar's wife, Dominique, and she was in Istanbul on the whim with Uncle Oscar.

Perry suggested Nina and Claude. They would be having their own Family Time, her mother said.

'Gran could come, then. She's actual family.'

'I don't think so,' said Perry's mother.

'Why not?'

'It wouldn't be restful.'

'Or healthy,' said Perry's father.

'Why?'

'I might have a heart attack,' he said.

'We could teach her how to play I Spy properly,' said Perry.

'Honora's not so good in public,' said Perry's father.

'Disinhibited,' he said. He said dis-in-*hib*-i-ted, and stretched his big lips like a horse chomping.

'We could take brunch to Santa Lucia, then,' said Perry. 'We could make the pancakes and take them with the maple syrup. And healthy fruit pieces.' *Healthy fruit pieces* might swing it, she thought.

But Perry's parents said Santa Lucia didn't have in-between meals like brunch. Their mealtimes were very regular, breakfast, lunch, dinner, with tea and biscuits in between, because that's what old people needed. And middle-aged people needed a break from all their responsibilities.

Perry went to her room and drew a picture of Gran wearing Perry's spectacles. The spectacles had thick lenses because Perry was as short-sighted as a mole. This was actually what Mr. Beardsley, the optician, had said when he tested her eyes.

On the other hand, Mr. Beardsley had added, moles were excellent tunnelers and they had a first-class sense of smell, especially the star-nosed mole. So all was not lost.

Perry had looked up the star-nosed mole in her *A to Z of World Animals and Insects*. It looked most unconventional.

Perry drew Gran's long face and the small spiked whiskers on her chin. She drew her silver swimming-

star-nosed mole
(condylura cristata)
nocturnal view

383

cap hair and her silver-white eyebrows, her sharp nose, her flicking eyes and her cross little mouth.

The portrait looked most witch-like until Perry added her magnifying spectacles. They had bright orange frames and blue spotted arms, so Gran changed from witch to circus clown, though there was no curly wig.

Under the picture Perry printed HONORA LEE

in capital letters even though Mrs. Warren, her homeroom teacher, and Mrs. Sonne *and* Haruka Homework were all very strict about lower case letters except at the beginning of names and sentences. She pinned the picture next to the Mr. Beardsley picture on her portrait board because that seemed right.

live long life

In February during M'n'M class Brita pulled a muscle in her lower back while she was demonstrating a low down bending movement and had to be taken home by her boyfriend, Jason, and his brother, Elliot. They made a seat with their big hands and carried weeping Brita out the door and down three flights of stairs.

Later that week all the parents received an email saying M'n'M class would be canceled for the rest of the term because Brita needed to take stock.

Taking stock was all very nice, said Perry's mother, but it was also a great nuisance because there didn't seem to be any other suitable after-school Thursday classes.

'I can do Music and Movement with Claude and Nina,' said Perry. She could do the music and Claude could do the movement. Claude loved dancing to Black Magic.

'Nina is better for art and fine motor skills,' said Perry's mother. 'I'll see about swimming again.'

But Nina wasn't able to take Perry to swimming on Thursdays because the only swimming pool with Thursday after-school lessons was on the other side of town and Nina didn't have a car on Thursdays. She shared a car with her friend Gregor and her days were Mondays, Wednesdays and Fridays.

'Sharing a car is ridiculous,' said Perry's mother.

'Though good for the environment,' said Perry's father.

'I should have put *car essential* in the job description.'

After much telephoning Perry's mother said she was Giving Up. She'd tried gym, trampoline, jazz ballet, After School Handcrafts and Beginner French, but there was nothing convenient. And contact sports were out of the question because of Perry's spectacles. And all the tennis classes were probably full.

'*Tennis, tennis,*' began Perry. '*A big fat menace.*' She chanted it in her hard foghorn voice.

'*Pat, Pat, the mean old rat.*'

Pat, the junior tennis coach at the Thorrington Tennis Club, had sighed extravagantly whenever he was showing Perry how to swing the racquet in slow sem-i-cir-*kills*. This was how he said it. Sem-i-cir-*KILLS*. Once he had squeezed her forearm slightly hard. And for two Saturdays in a row he had made

Perry and Deaf Raphael do volley board for the whole of class time.

'*I'm never, ever, ever. Gunna ever ever. Ever do tennis. In my live long life.*' Perry had composed this poem last year when tennis lessons were over. It didn't rhyme properly, but she didn't care. She chanted it in her foghorn voice whenever her parents mentioned tennis lessons.

'*Never, ever, ever. Gunna, never, ever. Ever gunna, gunna . . .*' chanted Foghorn Perry in the family room while her parents were talking about the Thursday Issue in the kitchen.

'*Going* to,' her mother called out. 'The word is go-*ing*.'

'I KNOW WHAT I CAN DO ON THURSDAYS,' shouted Perry. 'I ALREADY KNOW. I ALREADY *KNOW*!'

Her parents appeared suddenly, two stern statues in the door of the family room.

'What have we said about shouting?' said Perry's mother. Her voice was dangerously quiet.

'Don't do it,' said Perry, carelessly.

She was drawing a large picture of Santa Lucia in the summer with all the roses along the driveway and the hydrangeas and peonies and azaleas in Kaka garden where Gran was sometimes sitting when they arrived. Barbara, one of the caregivers, often walked Gran around the garden, naming the flowers for her. Perry could remember all the names. She was good at that sort of thing.

'Shouting is *not* the way to get attention,' said her mother.

Perry chose a light green crayon. She was going to draw the leaves of the big tree growing in the middle of Kaka garden. It was a ginkgo.

'Perry?'

'Yes,' said Perry.

'If you want to say something you come and talk quietly and face-to-face in a civilized way.'

'Grurg,' Perry said.

'Perry?'

'Raawk.'

'*Perry!*'

'Yes,' said Perry, meekly. It was hard to get the shape of the ginkgo leaves right. They were like the map of Australia, only not quite.

'So, what is it you think you can do on Thursdays?' said her mother. It was her patient voice now.

'Visit Gran,' said Perry. 'By myself.'

Her mother gave a snort. 'Don't be silly,' she said.

'Wait,' said Perry's father. He was holding up his hand, like a traffic warden.

'That is actually, *actually*, quite an interesting idea,' he said.

then

time waits for no man

On the first Thursday in March Perry walked home from the Ernle Clark School and then Nina and Claude walked her around the river, over the pedestrian crossing, through the fern reserve and across the little wooden bridge into the loop of the river and up the road to Santa Lucia. As they walked Perry kept an eye out for half asleep or half dead bumblebees. She had started a collection.

While Perry visited Gran, Nina and Claude walked further around the river to visit a friend. After an hour or so they walked back to Santa Lucia and picked up Perry.

'Good exercise, I suppose,' said Perry's mother. 'All the walking.'

She said this to Perry's father, in the kitchen, while Perry was in the family room. Her parents had had several talks about Perry visiting Gran, all in low and not very patient voices, but Perry could hear most of it anyway, because, though she was as short-sighted as a mole, her ears were as sharp as a spectacled fruit bat's.

'She really seems to like the old girl,' said Perry's father. He sounded surprised.

'Wouldn't you *know* it?' said her mother. And, 'What in the *world*?' And, 'For goodness' *sake*.'

That first Thursday Perry took baking to Santa Lucia because Gran had a sweet tooth; Perry had noticed this on Saturday visits. Gran gobbled up biscuits and muffins and scones. She liked ice cream, too, and chocolates and fruit jellies and brandy balls.

Nina had made Belgian Biscuits and Caramel Square and put them in her old Royal Wedding cake tin.

'How about I look after that?' said Audrey. She was an afternoon caregiver. 'Otherwise your Gran might want to eat the lot all in one go.'

Perry considered Audrey. She was very fat.

'You can't eat it,' she said.

'Wouldn't dream of it,' said Audrey, laughing fatly. 'Trust me.'

Perry wasn't so sure, but later Audrey brought cups of tea and a plate of the baking to the big community room where Perry sat with Gran and Gran's new best friend, Doris.

'Look what your granddaughter's made!' said Audrey.

'Nina made it, really,' said Perry.

'Goody, goody,' said Doris. She reached for a Belgian Biscuit.

'Whoops,' said Audrey, winking at Perry.

'I don't mind,' said Perry. 'Really. There's lots.'

'She's actually a boy,' said Gran in a loud whisper to Audrey.

'No I'm *not*,' said Perry. 'Perry can be a boy or a girl's name. It means nymph of the mountains.'

'Nymphs don't have spectacles,' said Gran.

'They might,' said Perry.

When the plate was empty Doris asked for more but Audrey said it would spoil her dinner.

'You are very unkind,' said Doris, sadly. 'Very, very unkind.' She shook her head slowly from side to side.

'Gotta be cruel to be kind,' said Audrey. 'Enjoy

your granddaughter, Honora.' She patted Gran. Her hand was big and weighty on Gran's long stick arm.

'I spy with my little eye,' said Gran, 'something beginning with *fat*.' She raised an eyebrow at Audrey.

'*Gran!*' Perry breathed.

'Out of the mouths of babes,' said Audrey, with a loud laugh. Her face was a great white wobble, little blue slits for eyes.

'Gran's forgotten how to play I Spy,' Perry told Audrey.

'I spy with my little eye something beginning with *cheeky*,' said Gran. She leaned over and whispered in Doris's ear.

'I'm *winning*.'

'Have fun!' said Audrey. She walked over to the other side of the community room to help Geoffrey, who sometimes fell sideways in his chair and called out, 'Nurse? Nurse?' in an old thin voice.

Gran stood up. Crumbs fell from her chest. Doris stood, too. She came up to Gran's shoulder. There was a spot of jam on her chin, like a shiny scab.

'Pupils any moment,' said Gran. 'Time waits for no man.'

'Time waits for no man,' echoed Doris.

Perry stood, too. She thought she might as well go with them.

a card, a pencil, a flower, a toothbrush

That evening Perry drew Audrey's laughing moon face. She drew Doris's tiny face and her mouth puckered up to blow a kiss. Doris blew a lot of kisses. Perry drew Sideways Geoffrey sloping like a wind-blown tree, the long gray cord dangling from his hearing aid. And she drew a picture of Paula, the senior nurse, clever and wise. Paula's hair was a straw-colored cloud around her head. It seemed to make a sighing sound when she moved quickly past, though it was hard to show this in the drawing.

'How was your visit with your Gran?' Paula had asked.

'She won't play I Spy properly,' said Perry.

'Honora prefers Improper I Spy,' said Paula. 'That way she can win.'

'She thought I was a pupil,' said Perry. 'So I let her.'

'Good on you,' said Paula.

'We did maths,' said Perry. 'We counted all the things in Gran's room. Then we put them into Sets. Gran said a card and a pencil and a flower and her toothbrush were all a Set, but a hairbrush wasn't.'

'Come back soon,' said Paula.

Perry made Paula beautiful in the picture. She tried to get exactly the right crayon mix for her eyes, which were golden brown, like the skin of a lion.

FIVE BUMBLEBEES

Perry made Sets of her portraits. She pinned the Paula picture beside the pictures of Nina and Claude. She put Doris beside Gran. She put Audrey beside Haruka Homework, and Sideways Geoffrey lying down on top of them so he would be comfortable.

a crack in the veranda

On the way to Santa Lucia the following Thursday Perry and Claude found five bumblebees. They weren't half asleep or half dead any more, they were fully deceased. Nina scooped them up with leaves, in case they still had stings, and put them in the yogurt pot they carried now for collecting.

This time Perry had brought banana cake. Gran and Doris ate two pieces each. Doris ate from the bottom up so the icing was saved until last. She licked the icing from her fingers and closed her eyes. She smiled slowly as the icing melted in her mouth.

Perry suggested a game of Improper I Spy.

'Molly doesn't know how to play,' said Gran. She often called Doris Molly.

'You just say, "I spy with my little eye",' said Perry to Doris, but now Doris was whispering to Jennifer, the cloth doll who wandered from chair to chair and room to room in Santa Lucia. Doris puckered her lips and blew Jennifer a delicate kiss.

'Enough of that,' said Gran, nudging Doris.

'*Kisses*,' said Gran scornfully.

'I spy with my little eye,' said Perry. 'Something beginning with Bosco!'

Gran squinted at her. 'How do you know Bosco?' She sounded most suspicious.

'You told me,' said Perry. This wasn't precisely true, but Gran wouldn't remember.

'You said he was your brother.'

'Of course he is,' said Gran. 'My naughty little brother!'

'Why is he naughty?'

'He runs away from school and hides under the house.'

Perry had looked under her house once, through a crack in the veranda. It was dark and cobwebbed and smelled like mushrooms. She'd been drawing on the veranda and a blue pencil had fallen down the crack.

'I'd rather go to school than go under the house,' she said.

Doris stood up suddenly, wobbly on her feet. 'I need to *go*.' She handed Jennifer to Gran. 'You tell her,' she said.

'What else did Bosco do?' Perry asked Gran. But Gran was standing too, ready to go. She flung Jennifer onto the sofa and hurried away.

Perry sighed. She wanted to know about Bosco.

And Vincent and Hughie. But conversations never lasted long at Santa Lucia. You had to keep following around and trying again. And again.

She followed Gran to the bedroom and tried to do Sets with her, but Gran wanted to lie down and read. Perry sat in the rocking chair and watched her. The book was an ABC, but Gran was reading it upside down.

'This isn't any good,' said Gran.

'I could read it to you,' said Perry.

'No thank you.'

'I spy with my little eye,' said Perry, hopefully.

'Something beginning with *peppermints!*' said Gran. She was off the bed in a flash, heading for the door. 'Pupils like peppermints.'

'P for pupils, P for peppermints,' said Gran as she plunged down the corridor.

'And P for Perry,' said Perry. She was walking fast to keep up.

'Who is Perry?'

'Just someone.'

Gran stopped in front of a door with the name Melvyn Broome. She turned the door handle and walked breezily into Melvyn Broome's room. Melvyn Broome wasn't there but she went to his chest of drawers anyway and opened the top drawer.

'But this is Melvyn Broome's room,' said Perry.

She smiled at the rhyme.

Gran took a packet of peppermints from the drawer and dug inside.

'I think they belong to Melvyn Broome,' said Perry. She was a little nervous.

Gran popped two large peppermints in her mouth and held out two to Perry.

'I don't think we should,' said Perry.

'P ish fur pruppamonts,' said Gran through her mouthful. She pushed the peppermints into Perry's hand.

'R is for Robber,' said Perry, closing her hand quickly into a fist.

þ r s ƒ m

'How was Honora Lee the Queen Bee?' said Perry's father at dinner.

'How come you don't call her Mum?' said Perry. And smiled at the rhyme.

'Never have, never will,' said her father. 'Called her Honora right from the cot. She told us to.'

'H for Honora,' said Perry.

'H for Handful,' said her father, 'or possibly Harridan,' and Perry's mother laughed into her broccoli.

'I'm going to do an alphabet book for Gran,' said Perry. 'She really likes the alphabet. We did

some today. We did P, R, S, F and M, and I made
Gran laugh.'

'That,' said Perry's father, 'is an achievement.'

S had been for Sweets and Sneaky, which Perry
had said when they were scurrying away from
Melvyn Broome's room.

F had been for Fingernail and Filing because
back in her bedroom Gran held out a finger to
show Perry a broken nail. Perry went to find
someone to cut the nail and returned with an
emery board from Loto. She fixed Gran's ragged
nail by herself.

'M is for Much Smoother,' said Perry, when she

had finished filing. It had taken a while because Gran's fingernails were thick and hard and took a long time to wear down, and Perry was rather clumsy with the emery board.

While Perry filed Gran whistled.

'I wish I could whistle,' said Perry. 'There should be whistling lessons instead of piano and clarinet.'

Gran stopped whistling for a moment and squinted at Perry.

'What is your name?'

'Perry,' said Perry, Very Patiently. 'P is for Perry. And don't say it's a boy's name.'

Gran began whistling again. It wasn't really a tune. It was more like a breathy birdcall.

'You have a most eccentric sense of melody,' said Perry.

That was when Gran had laughed, a sudden rat-a-tat, like gunshots on the tv. Perry jumped with fright.

lower case

The next Thursday Perry arrived at Santa Lucia with paper and felt pens and colored pencils and a stapler.

'You've got plans,' said Audrey. 'I can tell.' She was sitting outside the front entrance in a patch of sun, drinking coffee.

'We're making an ABC,' said Perry. 'Gran doesn't know it yet.'

'She does like her alphabet, your Gran. That's why we gave her that ABC.'

'She said it was I for Idiotic,' said Perry.

Audrey laughed in the middle of a gulp so the coffee went up her nose and all over her uniform. Which made her laugh even more.

'You're the laughingest person I ever met,' said Perry.

'Interesting word,' laughed Audrey. She dabbed at her uniform with a big red handkerchief.

Gran was standing under the ginkgo tree with Doris and Beverley, who could never get any words out. Beverley opened and shut her mouth,

but nothing ever came.

'Hello,' said Perry. Doris smiled and Beverley's lips moved like a goldfish's.

'Hello,' said Gran. 'Who are you?'

'Perry, of course. What are you doing?'

'Lessons, of course,' said Gran.

'What kind?'

'Questions afterwards.'

Doris came and stood right beside Perry, her jersey tickling Perry's bare arms. She smelled of tomato soup.

'Do you have biscuits?' said Doris.

'Yes,' said Perry. 'Yo Yos.'

Doris blew her a slow kiss.

Perry sat down at the table under the ginkgo tree

and spread out her art materials.

'I'm making an alphabet book,' she said. 'Who wants to help?'

'I'm far too busy,' said Gran. 'I have pupils all afternoon.'

'*I'm* a pupil,' said Perry. 'This book is for school. Starting with A. What can A be for?'

'*Anything*,' said Gran.

'Very funny,' said Perry, which was what her mother said when she didn't think something was funny at all.

She began stapling pages together for a book. How many letters were there in the alphabet? She started singing the alphabet song and counted on her fingers. 'Eh Bee See Dee Eee Eff Gee . . .'

'. . . Aitch, Eye, JayKay, Elemenopee,' sang Doris.

'Very good,' said Perry. But she had lost count after Kay. Never mind, she would just make fifty pages. There couldn't be more than fifty letters.

'Cue Are Ess Tee You Vee.' Doris had a high quavery voice. Beverley was singing too, but without any sound.

A ginkgo leaf spiraled down and rested on Perry's crayons. She placed it carefully in her pencil case. She would save it for Gee.

'Double Yoo Ex and Why and Zee.' Doris was conducting now. She was enjoying herself.

'Nowyouknowyourabctellyouwhatyouthinkofme,'
gabbled Gran over the top of Doris.

'The *End*,' said Gran, rather rudely. She sat down
on the slatted bench chair and folded her arms.

'It's Now *I* know *my* ABC, tell *me* what you think
of me,' said Perry.

'I think you're a cheeky little boy,' said Gran.

'Who's for afternoon tea?' Audrey came sailing
out the French doors with a tray of cups and Yo Yos.

'A is for *Audrey!*' said Perry, very pleased. 'The
laughingest person I know.' She began writing this
slowly on the first page of her book. She wrote in
lower case, because she was enjoying herself too.

out of order

On the way home Perry told Nina and Claude
about the first day of ABC.

'It's not really ABC,' she said. 'It's ADV, so far.
Gran does it out of order.'

'Sounds like Gran,' said Nina.

'And it takes me so long to write the sentences.'
'What is D?' said Nina.

'*My* D is for Dorothy,' said Perry.

Dorothy was new at Santa Lucia. She had been
there just two weeks and wanted to play the piano
all day long, even while the other residents were
watching TV.

If cricket was on Melvyn Broome and his friend Peter Pascoe got most annoyed with Dorothy; they shouted at her and waved their walking sticks, and Loto or Audrey or Bernard or Paula had to take Dorothy to another room to distract her. Dorothy had long pale fingers that reached out over the piano keys like probing tentacles. She hummed as she played. She didn't need any music, either. Perry thought she was *most* impressive.

'*D* is for Dorothy, who plays piano and makes Melvyn mad.'

'What is Gran's D for?'

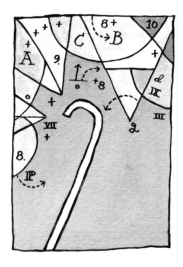

'Despot. Gran pointed at Audrey and said *D is for Despot,* because Audrey wouldn't let Doris have three Yo Yos. What *is* a despot?'

curiosity killed the cat

D was for Doris, too, of course. Doris had said, *D is for Doris, D is for Doris.* She had come and stood right by Perry and droned, *D is for Doris, D is for Doris.*

'Don't be a Drama Queen, Molly,' said Gran, which had made Doris cry and Audrey took Doris for a walk to comfort her. But Perry had scribbled *D is for Drama Queen* because she thought it would make a good picture.

'Then Gran said *V is for Victor,*' Perry told her parents at dinnertime. 'But when I said who is Victor, she said curiosity killed the cat.'

'It's hard to have conversation,' she added.

'More like impossible,' said her father.

'Who's Victor anyway?' said her mother.

'Probably a pupil,' said Perry's father. 'Maybe a horse. They had so many horses. Honora was mad about them. She was always going on about those old nags. I bet he was a horse.'

So, on the V page Perry drew a horse. Horses were tricky, especially if you tried to make them gallop, which was best, Perry thought. She wanted Gran galloping because Gran was rather like a

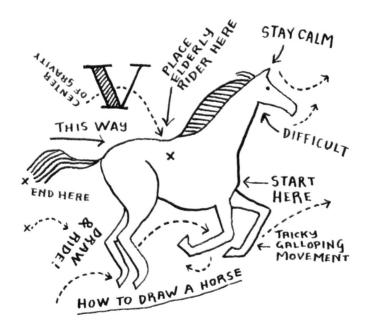

STAY CALM

PLACE ELDERLY RIDER HERE

CENTER OF GRAVITY

THIS WAY

DIFFICULT

END HERE

START HERE

DRAW & RIDE!

TRICKY GALLOPING MOVEMENT

HOW TO DRAW A HORSE

charging horse. She did everything fast — walking, eating, getting out of a chair, going through a door. It was why she often had bruises: she moved so fast she banged into things a great deal. Audrey called her Mrs. Break Neck.

Perry drew Victor the horse in full gallop, with Gran in the saddle. She drew a riding helmet on Gran and a plaster on her cheek where her current bruise was, big as a plum.

The next Thursday Karl was sitting under the ginkgo with Gran and Loto.

Karl stared at Perry. 'Are you da girl wid da vebbrrick zamples?' Karl had gold in his front tooth. He always looked worried.

'No,' said Perry, though she wasn't sure what Karl had said.

'This is Honora's granddaughter, Karl,' said Loto. 'She's making a book.'

'An ABC,' said Perry. 'It's a project. I have to do it by the third term.' She showed them *D is for Drama Queen*. She had drawn a stage and a towering queen with red glitter all over her gown. The Queen had a tiara and a small face like Doris.

'That's rather magnificent,' said Loto.

'Ven vill da girl wid da vebbrrick zamples com?' said Karl.

'Karl was a tailor, you know,' said Loto. 'He made beautiful suits and dresses. He had a very successful business, didn't you, Karl?' Loto took Karl's hand and massaged his fingers.

'Hard-working hands, eh Karl?'

Karl frowned.

'Shall we go and see about those fabric samples?' said Loto. 'C'mon, Karl. We'll see if they've arrived and you can sign for them.' Loto helped Karl to his feet and led him inside.

'Bonkers,' said Gran to Perry.

'That's not very nice, Gran,' said Perry.

'Nice, nice,' said Gran, screwing up her mouth.
'What's nice? I haven't got time for *nice*.'

Perry opened her book to a fresh spread and
smoothed down the pages. She was feeling most
organized.

'Time for B! B is for . . .'

'Bonkers,' said Gran.

'B is for *Beverley* and *Bernard* and *Barbara*,' said
Perry, very firmly. She was going to have everyone
at Santa Lucia in the book.

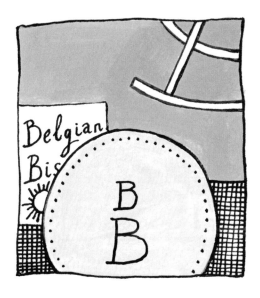

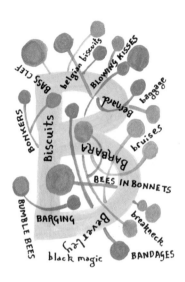

'Where are the biscuits?' There was Doris, coming through the French doors. She had been to the Santa Lucia hairdresser. Her hair was fluffed up like a dandelion clock, and her lips were pink with lipstick.

'B is for *Biscuits*! Very good, Doris. You look nice.' Doris blew a slow and delicate kiss and Perry pretended to catch it on her cheek.

'And B is for Blowing Kisses . . .'

Perry wrote *B is for blowing kisses. Doris does it delicately.*

'Have you got a B, Gran?'

'Only in my bonnet,' said Gran. 'Hardy ha ha.' Gran was sitting with her arms and legs crossed very tight indeed. She had a black sandal on her left foot and a blue slipper on her right. Also, a bandage on her calf.

B is for bandages and bruises because Gran bashes into things.

'Afternoon tea, ladies?' Paula had the tea tray today. Her big hair was tied up in an orange scarf; she had beads of many colors around her neck. Perry thought she looked *most* magnificent.

'Here's Lady Muck,' said Gran.

'And good afternoon to you, too, Honora Lee. Perry's spoiling you again, I see.' Perry smiled at the rhyme and took some Ginger Crunch.

'Who's Perry?' said Gran.

'How's the ABC going?' asked Paula. She sat down beside Perry.

'Slowly,' said Perry. 'And not in the right order. We're up to C.'

'*See how the Fates their gifts allot,*' sang Gran.

'—not that See,' said Perry. '*C!*'

'*For A is happy — B is not!*
Yet B is worthy, I dare say,
Of more prosperity than A!'

Doris clapped and Gran gave a little bow. She was almost smiling.

'You have an amazing memory for songs, Honora,' said Paula.

'Practice,' said Gran. 'P is for *Practice makes Perfect.*'

'*Ceeeeee,*' growled Perry.

largo and allegro

In April, James's clarinet pupils were giving a
concert. Perry practiced every evening to make
perfect. Her mother sat on the green sofa,
embroidering and counting, One and *two* and, One
and *two* and, while Perry played *Go tell Aunt Rhody*.

'What a mournful tune,' said Perry's mother.
'Don't you have a more cheerful piece?'

'We tried a cheerful piece,' said Perry, 'but it was
Allegro. *Allegro* is too hard. I'm best at *Largo*.' She
made a special moaning sound on the clarinet to
show that the old gray goose was truly dead. It wasn't
in the music, but her mother didn't know that.

'Can Gran come to the concert?' Perry asked
her father. He was sitting at his computer, typing
very *Largo*.

'Too tricky,' said her father. He was going to
Hong Kong to talk about Sustainable Business and
couldn't come to the concert.

'Who's Aunt Rhody anyway?' Perry asked.

'Someone whose goose is deceased.'

'Where do you think she lived?'

'On a farm probably.'

'Gran lived on a farm.'

'Her father had a farm, yes.'

'Did they have geese?'

'Perry.' Her father lifted his hands off the

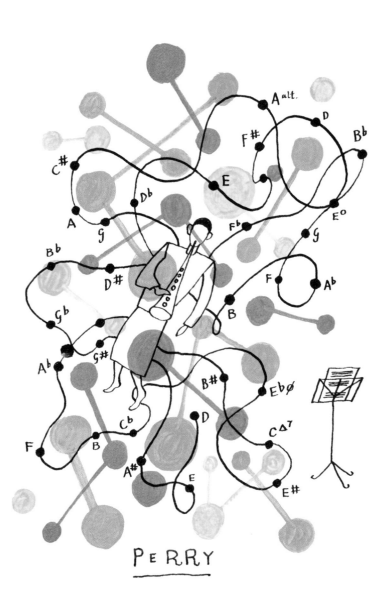

PERRY

keyboard. 'I need to finish this proposal before I go to bed.'

Perry wrote *C is for Clarinet Concert* in Gran's ACB and the next Thursday she took her clarinet to Santa Lucia and gave a special recital to Gran, Doris, Beverley, Paula, Loto, Audrey, Bernard, Barbara, Melvyn Broome, Peter Pascoe, Dorothy and Karl.

The concert was outside under the ginkgo, though there were no leaves on the tree any more. They had all fallen off in one day, Loto said. That's what ginkgos did. They shed their leaves quickly. *Allegro.*

'Winter's coming,' said Melvyn Broome, a little sadly.

'You'll miss the cricket, Melvyn, won't you?' said Paula.

'Melvyn played cricket every Saturday,' she told Perry. 'Tell Perry your best figures, Melvyn?'

'5 for 14 off 20,' said Melvyn.

'Very good,' said Perry. She didn't have a clue what it meant. She gave an experimental blow on her clarinet.

'5 for 14 off 20,' said Melvyn Broome again.

'*Well* done,' said Paula.

'5 for 14 off 20!' shouted Melvyn Broome.

'Give the man a beer!' whooped Peter Pascoe.

'Quiet now everyone,' said Paula, 'there's going to be music.'

They all clapped *Go tell Aunt Rhody*, even Gran.

'Not as silly as you look,' said Gran.

'Did you have a goose on your farm, Gran?'

'I spy with my little eye,' said Gran, 'something beginning with dribble.' She pointed to the bottom of Perry's clarinet.

'It's my *breath*,' said Perry. 'It turns to water.'

'Crying,' said Doris.

a walking stick is not a weapon

'How was the concert?' Perry's father asked. He was back from Hong Kong and standing very straight against the wall. His back was sore from so much sitting on planes and in lecture theaters.

Perry was doing a portrait of Melvyn Broome for the W page. Melvyn was tall and thin and his skin was very smooth, much smoother than most of the others at Santa Lucia, who had lines and ditches and spots all over. Melvyn looked like Woody in *Toy Story*.

Perry drew a hat on Melvyn's head. She had seen a photo of Melvyn in his cricket clothes and floppy white hat. She had seen it when Gran took her to rob more peppermints.

'The concert for Gran was good. I didn't get nervous at all.'

'Apparently the real concert was good, too. Mum says you've improved.'

Perry wrote *W is for Walking stick, which Melvyn uses as a Weapon*.

Melvyn had been extremely cross when he

discovered Gran robbing his peppermint drawer. He shouted Thief! Thief! though his expression didn't change; and he had smacked Gran on the top of her leg with his walking stick. Gran had yelped in pain, she had folded over like Jennifer-the-Cloth-Doll, clutching at her leg.

Perry ran for Paula and Paula came running, too. She stood between Gran and Melvyn Broome and calmed everything down.

'A walking stick is not a weapon, Melvyn,' said Paula, most sternly.

'We must all respect other people's privacy,' she told Gran. 'And their property.'

'But, Gran won't remember that,' said Perry. She watched while Paula wrote it all down in the Incident Book.

'No,' said Paula, 'it's sad to say. And neither will Melvyn. So we'll have to be more vigilant.'

'And get Gran some peppermints,' said Perry.

small broken meow

The next Thursday Perry arrived with her art materials, three newly discovered bumblebees (deceased), the ACB, a jumbo packet of peppermints, a tin of Hokey Pokey biscuits and her origami zoo to show Gran. She had two new animals, a squirrel and a fox, because Haruka

Homework was so pleased with her writing progress.

It was raining. Perry sat with Gran and Doris and Jennifer-the-Cloth-Doll in the peacock cushion living room. She spread everything out on the coffee table and opened up the ACB.

'What letter shall we do today?' Perry had given up on an orderly alphabet. She was going to let Gran decide.

But Gran was unexpectedly quiet today. She just sucked the peppermints and sat staring at the origami zoo. Doris wanted to unfold the fox and the tiger, so Perry had given the animals to Gran for safekeeping. They were lined up on the arm of the sofa and Gran smacked Doris's hand away if she reached for them. She smacked quite gently.

'Have you got a letter, Gran?'

'*Some*body's taken my letters,' said Gran. She narrowed her eyes.

'An alphabet letter,' said Perry. 'ABC. There are twenty-six and we've only done fifteen.'

'I have no letters from Noel, not a one.'

'Just say any letter.'

'Who is she?' whispered Gran to Doris.

'She's the *biscuit* girl,' Doris whispered back.

So Perry did *Q is for Quiet*, which it hardly ever was at Santa Lucia. There was nearly always noise: cups and plates and pots clattering in the kitchen,

Dorothy playing *You'll Never Walk Alone*, toilets flushing, the calump-thump calump-thump of walking frames down the corridor, visitors laughing, doors banging, Loto explaining to Karl about his fabric samples, Barbara calling out the directions at exercise time, Uta's strange growling groan as she went from room to room looking and looking for who knew what.

But sometimes when Perry was concentrating hard on her lower case letters or shading a picture, and Gran and Doris weren't bickering, and the television was muted, and Karl was having a lie down, it might become suddenly quiet; and then — just for a moment — you could hear the sounds behind the sounds, the sounds of quiet: the brief, piercing song of the bellbird who visited Kaka garden; the musical squeak of Gran's rocking chair; Paula pulling the brush through little Olga's long white hair; Peter Pascoe's teaspoon clinking around and around and around in his teacup; or a small broken meow from Topaz the Santa Lucia ginger cat, who often woke from a long nap and didn't know quite where he was.

glurg floik qwoonk

'Who is Noel?' Perry asked.

She had done her clarinet practice and her

piano practice and even her homework sheet. Now she was drawing a portrait of Eric, the manager of Santa Lucia.

Eric sat much of the day in front of his computer, doing the accounts and the rosters and talking on the phone. He had a lot of meetings in his office. Sometimes he walked around the building with men in overalls or he toured the garden with Max the Santa Lucia gardener. But occasionally he came and sat with everyone in the community room. He liked a chat. He liked afternoon tea. He liked Nina's baking.

On Easter Saturday Eric had arrived with marshmallow Easter eggs for everyone. There were enough for visitors, too. In the ACB Perry had written *E is for Eric and his excellent Easter Eggs.*

Perry drew Eric at his computer, glimpsed through the office window. She drew his half-smile and his chewed fingernails. She drew him giving a little salute, which he often did when he saw Perry.

'Noel?' said Perry's father.

He was lying on the sofa with a cold cloth over his face. He had been to Kuala Lumpur and back again all in five days and it had made him Weary and Fractious, he said.

Perry's mother was at Book Group. She had taken an Eggless, Butterless Cake because there

were Vegans in her Book Group. Nina said it should be called Tasteless, Pointless Cake.

'Only Noel I know is my old Dad,' said Perry's father, his voice blurry under the cold cloth.

'Gran hasn't had a *single* letter from him.'

'Not surprising since he's been dead and buried for twenty years.'

'Gran's *most* annoyed with him.'

'Hah! Wha—' But Perry's father whooped too hard and unexpectedly sucked in the cold cloth. There was an interesting series of choking and gulping and swearing sounds before he spoke again.

'She's going to write to him anyway,' said Perry. 'I'm helping her. Do you like my Eric?'

She was pleased with Eric's portrait. His crumpled checked shirt was just right. Perry was planning to rearrange the notice board and put Eric and Paula at the top. They were like the mother and father of Santa Lucia.

'Old Eric, eh? He looks like an exhausted Labrador. What a job.'

'We should *get* an exhausted Labrador. It wouldn't make a racket or a mess,' Perry said. 'I like Eric.'

'How's the crazy abecedary?'

'*What?*'

'You mean: 'I beg your pardon?'

'Glurg,' said Perry. 'Floik.' She pulled her

spectacles to the end of her nose and crossed her eyes at her father. She had tried this in front of her bedroom mirror. It was surprisingly frightening.

'Stop that,' he said. 'You know your mother hates it. It is a word for alphabet. Abecedary is a word for alphabet.'

'Qwoooonk,' said Perry in her foghorn voice, still cross-eyed.

'Time for bed, I think,' said her father, briskly.

social animals

In the first week of May there was an outbreak of norovirus at Santa Lucia.

'Stomach cramps,' said Perry's mother. 'Temperatures. Vomiting, etcetera.'

'Is Gran sick?' said Perry.

'Honora is fine so far, but no one can visit because it's highly contagious. Everyone's quarantined.'

'Doris won't like that one bit,' said Perry. 'She likes lots of visitors. She's a social animal.' Perry had heard Barbara and Loto discussing this.

'Like ants,' Perry added. 'They're social animals, too.' She had read this in her *A to Z of World Animals and Insects*. 'And bees. They live in colonies.' She was reading a lot about bees lately.

Perry's mother laughed. She had nearly finished

the moss green cushion and it had put her in a good mood. Her needle was speeding through the fabric.

'Can we still go on Saturday?'

'Probably not.'

'When can we go?'

'When it's all over.'

'Will it be over next Monday?'

'I don't know.'

'Next Tuesday?'

'*Perry.*'

'I'm just asking.'

'Well, I'm not a doctor, so I can't say, can I?'

'You're a psychologist.'

'Perry.' Her mother's voice was heading towards dangerously quiet.

'What good *is* a psychologist?'

'I sometimes wonder,' said her mother. She tied a slow knot in her russet colored embroidery cotton.

'It's nearly the third term,' said Perry. 'This Outbreak couldn't of come at a worst time.'

'Couldn't *have*,' said her mother.

sticky end

So, the following Thursday Perry had to find other things to do.

She read about the Tasmanian Tiger in her *A to Z of World Animals and Insects.*

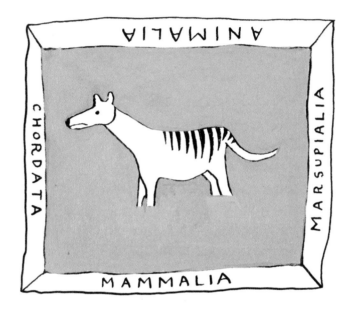

She composed a new extra grim version of Black
Magic for Claude to dance to.

She rearranged her deceased bumblebee
collection into a different pattern. There were
twenty-two bees now. Perry had laid them out on a
piece of faded fabric from her mother's sewing
basket, though her mother had complained it was a
most peculiar and macabre collection for a nine-
year-old girl and she didn't like it one bit. But
Perry liked to look at the bees. She checked them

regularly. She had drawn several pictures of them. Their shapes changed over time, their yellows and blacks faded. The first bees she had found were curled up now and felt a little crisp when you touched them. It was most interesting. Claude liked the bee collection too. He had helped spot a lot of them.

After that Perry worked on the ACB anyway. Claude colored in the letters using her top-grade Derwent Colorsoft Pencils.

Perry wrote *O is for Outbreak* and *Q is for Quarantine* and drew a picture of Eleanor clutching her stomach. Eleanor was Perry's least favorite person at Santa Lucia. Once when Perry had been passing her chair Eleanor had grabbed Perry's wrist and *pinched* her. She had cackled with ugly pleasure, like a cartoon witch.

Gran had bustled over to tell Eleanor off but Eleanor had grabbed Gran's wrist with her other hand. She had held them both there, a witch with super powers.

'That'll be quite enough, you old baggage!' Gran said, trying to unclamp Eleanor's fingers with her own bent and bony ones. 'You'll come to a Sticky End!'

Cackle, cackle, went Eleanor. She gripped their wrists tight until Audrey came and sorted it out.

'Worse than school, isn't it?' said Audrey.

'About the same,' said Perry. Her wrist hurt for several days.

She added *Baggage* to the Bee list, which was getting rather long, and *Sticky End* to the Esses. She thought about the bruise she had got from the pinch and drew a long spurt of vomit coming from Eleanor's mouth. She let Claude color it in with seven different pencils.

oh for a thousand tongues to sing

On Saturday Santa Lucia was still in quarantine. The norovirus had passed but visitors were discouraged. Unless it was urgent. Perry's father said he didn't want to risk it.

'But it *is* urgent,' said Perry. 'I've only got three weeks.'

'For what?'

Perry considered giving her father the cross-eyed look.

'I *told* you,' she said.

'Told me what?'

'About the ACB,' said Perry.

'Can't you do it by yourself?'

'I need Gran. And the others. It's a group ACB. We're social animals.'

'How about a spot of piano practice?' said her

father. 'I'll listen while I type. I'll type in time to your beat.'

'You'll come to a Sticky End,' growled Perry.

But she practiced anyway. Perry had graduated to *Faber Piano Adventures Gold Star Performance Level* **Two** after several weeks of practicemakesperfect. She was feeling most pleased with the piano. Gabriel said it was a great leap forward.

The first piece in the new book was *Scaling Mount Everest*. The notes climbed up and up, winding slowly to the top. Perry tried to picture the snowdrifts and the climbers' heavy packs and boots and ropes, as Gabriel had suggested. She played *Lento* and *Maestoso* and *Coldly* because that's how mountain climbers would go. She planned to play it twenty times to makeperfect, but pretty soon her father began to howl like a gray wolf. He begged for a change of tune.

'And absolutely not Black Magic,' he said. 'Do you have a piece called Silence?'

'Very funny,' said Perry. 'Can I ring Gran?'

'Why?'

'I want to talk to her?'

'What about? Can't you wait till Thursday?'

'No,' said Perry. She watched her father at his computer, plodding over the keys like a heavy-booted mountaineer. He had terrible posture, her

Scaling Mt Everest

mother said. Perry's mother had excellent posture because she did Pilates. She was at Pilates right now.

'So, can I?'

'With you in a minute,' said her father, staring hard at the screen. 'Give me a minute.'

Minutes were the strangest amounts of time, Perry often thought; sometimes they took a whole morning. She went to the family room phone and pressed 9, which was the Direct Dial for Santa Lucia.

Stephen answered the phone. He was mostly a weekend nurse. Perry liked Stephen. His head was shaven and shiny; he had teeth rather like the wolverine in her *A to Z of World Animals and Insects*.

'It's Perry,' she said. 'Can I speak to my Gran?'

'If I can find her,' said Stephen. 'Take a walk with me.'

'Is she all right?' asked Perry. 'Has she been sick?' Stephen was taking her by phone down the hall and into the community room. She could hear the TV.

'She's as fit as the proverbial fiddle,' said Stephen. 'And crabby as an old apple. They've all got cabin fever, here.'

'My mother said it was norovirus.'

'Cabin fever's the bit that comes after. No one's been out for a week, and no visitors have come in.'

'Anyone seen Honora?' he called.

Perry pictured everyone in their different chairs:

Melvyn Broome and Peter Pascoe with their walking sticks. Sideways Geoffrey who often had to watch the television at an angle. Eleanor shooting out her claw to grab passers-by. Doris whispering to Jennifer-the-Cloth-Doll. Karl fretting about fabric samples. Dorothy swaying at the piano, pretend-playing on the closed lid because the TV was going. Perry wished she were there.

'She's not in the living room,' said Stephen. 'We'll try the bedroom. How are you, anyway?' He was very friendly.

'I'm good,' said Perry. 'But I'm worried about my ACB.'

'How's that going? You got an X yet? X is always hard. And Z.'

'No, I haven't,' said Perry. 'That's why I'm worried.'

'Don't panic,' said Stephen. 'You can always have zizzzzes for Z. You know, sleeping. There's a lot of that round here.' He was walking through the dining room and kitchen now. Perry could tell by the sounds; it was the raucous music of cutlery and pot lids and the big oven doors banging.

'Will I be able to come on Thursday?'

'For sure. All back to normal on Monday.'

'I need some Os before then. Do you have an O?'

'*Oh dear, where can Honora be?*' Stephen sang. He was

a good singer — he was in a choir. His choir had given a concert one weekend at Santa Lucia and Stephen had sung a solo.

'Hardy ha ha,' said Perry. 'You know what O I mean.'

'*O Come All Ye Faithful*,' sang Stephen in a fake bass voice. He was in the bedroom corridor now, the sounds had changed again.

'Or we have, *O Little Town of Bethlehem* . . .' Perry could hear doors being opened. Gran didn't always go to her own room, Perry knew. Sometimes she got into other beds. No one really minded, except Melvyn Broome.

'Or, how could I forget? *O Christmas Tree! O Christmas Tree!*' Stephen bellowed merrily as he opened and shut doors. 'Or! *O Holy Night!* There's a surprising number of Christmas Carols beginning with O, when you think about it . . . *And*, here she is! Honora Lee, hanging out in Mary Foley's room. Quite comfortable there, Honora?'

'What the devil do you want?' said Gran. Perry heard her quite clearly.

'Nicely, please,' said Stephen.

'Is Mary Foley there?' Perry asked.

'No, her family have taken her to morning tea at the Garden Center,' said Stephen. 'Wait! I've thought of another one . . . *O Danny Boy, the pipes the pipes are calling* . . . Honora, phone for you. It's Perry.'

'Who the devil's Perry?' said Gran, into the
phone. Perry could just see her, scowling.

'Your *granddaughter*,' said Perry severely. 'I've been
missing you, Gran.'

'Not today, thank you,' said Gran.

'I'm doing the ACB,' said Perry. 'We're up to O.
What do you think O should be for? I can only
think of orange juice. And Stephen keeps saying
Christmas Carols.'

'Christmas,' said Gran. 'Spare me.'

'O for . . .' said Perry, hopefully.

'*Oh for a muse of fire that would ascend* . . .' said Gran.
'William Shakespeare.'

'Oh,' said Perry. She'd heard of William
Shakespeare. 'Okay. I'll put that. Could you say it
again? Could you say it slowly? Oh. For. A . . .' She
wrote as quickly as possible on the telephone notepad.

'*Oh for a thousand tongues to sing, my Great Redeemer's
praise*,' sang Gran. 'Charles Wesley. He wrote six
thousand hymns. Good bye.' And Gran put the
phone down. But it wasn't switched off and Perry
could hear thumps and bangs and slams through
the muffle of Mary Foley's bedspread.

She could imagine exactly what Gran was doing:
throwing back the covers and half-falling out of
Mary Foley's bed, stomping across the floor in bare

OH FOR A MUSE OF FIRE
THAT WOULD ASCEND...

feet, or mismatched slippers, charging down the
corridor until . . . until she was somewhere else
and all her noises had faded.

Perry listened for a few seconds to the silence in
Mary Foley's bedroom and then pressed the End
button. She stared at the scribble on the telephone
notepad. It didn't make any sense.

'Okay,' said her father, coming into the family
room. 'Your Obedient Servant. You want to ring
Honora?'

'Who the devil is Charles Wesley?' said Perry.

vital, vital

Perry went to Santa Lucia every day the next week. It was the holidays and she was making the most of it. There were no music lessons, there was no After School Tutoring, there was nothing but Nina and Claude for two weeks. And a visit to Gran every afternoon. It was perfect. Perry had convinced her mother. She had said it was vital, *vital* for the ACB project. Vital was a word her father used a lot.

Perry's mother had opened her mouth to argue and then shut it again — just like Beverley. She was too busy to argue. She was helping organize a psychologists' conference.

Everyone was delighted to see Perry.

'Welcome back!' said Audrey. 'Boy, did we miss you.'

'Really?' said Perry.

'Of course. You're a fixture round here. If it's Thursday it must be Perry. *And* her baking,' said Audrey. She gave one of her heavy winks.

'It's actually Monday,' said Perry. 'And I'm coming every day for two weeks.'

'With baking?'

'Hardy ha,' said Perry. 'Probably.'

Nina had made Shortbread; she said it would be light and undemanding on recently upset tummies. Perry and Claude had helped. They decorated the tops of the biscuits with fork marks, three rows of

four, and sneaked pieces of dough when Nina wasn't looking.

It was a cold day. Gran was sitting under the leafless ginkgo wearing a coat, a scarf and a woolen hat with a pompom. Her arms were folded tight across her chest. Paula was sitting beside Gran, jiggling her legs up and down.

'Hello, hello,' said Paula. 'Someone won't go inside.'

'What's wrong with a bit of cold?' said Gran.

'Pneumonia?' said Paula.

'Toughen up,' said Gran. She blew her breath out in a huff and almost smiled at the small cloud she made.

'Nice coat,' said Paula. 'Nice *hat*.'

Perry had a new merino jacket and a hat. No pompom. The jacket and hat were bright orange like the arms of her glasses. Perry's mother had wanted forest green, but Perry liked to be matching.

'I can work out here with Gran,' said Perry. 'I'm *extremely* warm.'

'We don't want you getting sick, either,' said Paula.

'I'm Tough,' said Perry, spreading out her materials and turning to the T page of the ACB. 'T is for *Tough*.'

Gran snorted. She rolled her eyes at Perry.

'And for tetchy,' said Paula, softly.

'What's tetchy?' whispered Perry.

'No whispering!' Gran shouted, making them both jump.

'I do beg your pardon, Honora,' said Paula. 'That was rude of us.'

'It means irritable,' she said to Perry. 'Peevish. Testy. Grumpy.'

'Speak for yourself,' said Gran. She did look grumpy, though, Perry thought, or more grumpy than usual; a grumpy little bird all weighed down by heavy plumage.

'I know you're missing Doris,' said Paula. She put her arm around Gran.

'Where's Doris?' said Perry. She put down her pencil.

'Doris,' said Paula, carefully, 'has had to leave. She's had to go to hospital care. The virus knocked her about.'

'But that's terrible,' said Perry. *T for Terrible*. It really was.

'It is very sad,' said Paula. 'We're all missing her, but Honora's really pining.'

'But won't she come back?' said Perry. She couldn't believe it.

'I don't think so,' said Paula. She gave Perry's hand a squeeze.

Perry was silent and her pencils still. She looked

sideways at Gran, at her long face, her bristly chin.

'You're staring,' said Gran.

'Poor Gran,' said Perry. She reached up and kissed Gran on her chilly cheek.

'Huh,' said Gran, batting Perry away. 'Kisses.'

t is for tender-hearted

Perry and Nina and Claude walked home along the riverbank. They walked *Molto Lento* because that was Claude's speed. And they stopped often to look at the river, at the ducks, or to pick up leaves, or say hello to dogs and their owners. There were no bees around, half-witted or asleep or deceased. It was too cold now.

'Gran *is* tetchy,' Perry told Nina, 'but she was kind, too. She helped Doris with her clothes, she helped her do up her buttons and her shoes. And she helped her at dinner. She tied Doris's bib, and then she untied it after dessert. Paula told me.'

'So really, she's T for tender-hearted,' said Nina. 'Deep down.'

Deep, deep down, thought Perry.

'And now she doesn't have anyone to help,' said Nina.

'She could help *me* with the ACB—'

'Did she have a T?' Nina asked.

'Not really,' said Perry. 'She just sang *Tea for Two and Two for Tea*, and then she ate four pieces of Shortbread. Paula didn't even try and stop her.'

possibly chaotic

'How goes the anarchic alphabet?' said Perry's father at dinner on Wednesday night.

'Whatdoesanarchicmean?' said Perry, in an almost foghorn voice. She said it through a mush of chicken and carrot and beans, though talking with a full mouth was deplorable manners, her mother said. It was her father's fault, Perry thought. He'd asked her the question. It would have been deplorable manners to ignore him.

'Lacking order,' said her father. 'Lawless. Possibly chaotic.'

Perry swallowed. She made a great effort.

'It's going good—'

'Going well,' said her mother. Perry ignored her.

'—but Gran isn't being very cooperative,' (Cooperative was a favorite word of Mrs. Sonne's)—

'What's new?' said her father and mother together.

'—because,' said Perry in a dangerously quiet voice, 'she is feeling very sad about Doris. She's *pining*.'

Her parents didn't say anything to that. They busily ate their chicken and carrot and beans. Perry listened to the chewing and the clicking of their jaws.

'We still need U Z X Y and J,' she said. 'I'm trying J tomorrow.'

'Can you actually remember how to say the alphabet in the correct order?' Perry's father asked.

'Probably,' said Perry. 'But who wants to?'

how do you practice a table?

Gran was in the dining room with Audrey when Perry arrived the next day. There was a stack of folders on the table and another stack on the floor. Audrey tried to find quiet places to write her reports, but Gran was never far away.

'Better,' said Gran. She was peering at Audrey's notes. 'You're improving. Slowly.'

'Kind of you to say so,' said Audrey.

'Hello Gran,' said Perry.

'Shush,' said Gran. 'People are concentrating.'

'Or trying to,' said Audrey.

Gran rolled her eyes.

'Paperwork, paperwork,' muttered Audrey. 'The curse of the health system.'

'Is Gran helping you?'

'You could say that.'

'This girl,' said Gran, pointing with her bent finger, 'is a *wretched* speller.'

Audrey laughed. 'This girl ain't been a girl for a few decades now, darling. But you're right. Can't spell to save myself!'

'*I* before *e* except after *c*!' Gran blurted. '*Rhy*thm helps your *two hips* move! R! H! Y! T! H! M!'

Perry and Audrey stared.

'I'm *rough* and *tough* and that's *enough*!' sang Gran, banging the table in time to the rhyme. 'What is the *weight* of the *freight* on car number *eight*?! There's a *hen* in *when*! There's a *hen* in *when*!'

Gran looked at them expectantly. She had a Band-Aid on her ear, Perry noticed, and a small red bump on her forehead.

'Well?' said Gran.

'A hen in when,' said Audrey, at last. 'I'll remember that.'

'See that you do,' said Gran.

'I'm ready for *my* lesson now,' said Perry. She sat down at the neighboring table and spread out the ACB materials.

'Come and sit with me, Gran.' Perry patted the seat next to her.

'Can you spell?' said Gran, suspiciously.

'Not very well,' said Perry, smiling at the rhyme. 'I'm up to J. But I need help. J is for . . .'

'Japonica juice makes jolly good jelly,' said Gran, promptly. She stood up and came over to Perry's table. '*Joan Jack*son has *jet* black jewels.'

'That is so good,' said Perry. She wrote *J is for Jelly* as quickly as she could. They often had it for dessert at Santa Lucia. She wrote *J is for Jewels*. Dorothy had jewels. She wore heavy necklaces that sparkled in the sunlight; her bracelets tinkled accompaniments when she swayed at the piano.

'Who is Joan Jackson?' said Perry.

'Never heard of her,' said Gran. She sat down beside Perry with a thump. 'Now, what about your Tables? Have you been practicing your Tables?'

'Tables?' said Perry, puzzled. 'How do you practice a *table*?' She played pretend *Scaling Mount Everest* on the tabletop.

'Two twos are four,' chanted Audrey, 'two threes are six.' She dropped a folder onto the floor. 'Five down, fifteen to go.'

'Five down, fifteen to go, that's a jolly odd Table,' said Gran.

Perry wrote *J is for Jolly Odd*, because that's what most

conversations at Santa Lucia were, including this one.

'There's no one here beginning with J, is there?' said Perry.

'There . . . *Was* . . . Judith,' said Audrey. She spoke slowly, her lips making odd shapes, she was concentrating on her writing. 'But . . . That was . . . Before your time.'

My time, thought Perry, pleased. 'You mean Gran's time.'

'Spose,' said Audrey. 'But you two kind of go together.'

'We go together, Gran.' Perry nudged Gran, and tried a wink like Audrey's.

'That'll be the frosty Friday,' said Gran.

'And we had John,' Audrey continued. 'He was such a lovely gentleman. An actual *gentle* man. It was so sad when he passed away, we—'

'Where's that Molly got to?' said Gran, standing up violently. The chair banged over behind her.

'Hey, hey, Mrs. Break Neck!' said Audrey. 'Take it *slowly*, now. *Slow-ly*.' She heaved her big body up and bent over wheezily to pick up the chair.

'Doris is over at Heathcote now, dear little thing.' Audrey took Gran's arm. 'Shall we go and see about some afternoon tea? We'll check out what Perry's brought today.'

'Who's Perry?' said Gran.

'Your *grand*daughter!' called Perry, as Gran
rushed at the dining room doors.

'I spy with my little eye something beginning
with *shouting*!' shouted Gran.

Perry sat in the echoing dining room looking at
the J page. She selected some pencils and began to
draw shapely jellies: red, yellow, green, purple; and
as she drew she thought about Judith Before Her
Time and John the Gentle Man. She thought about
Passing Away. She would put that on the P page, she
decided. It seemed to happen quite often at Santa
Lucia.

She thought about Doris over at Heathcote

Hospital now and wondered if she was missing everyone at Santa Lucia. She thought about Doris saving the icing till last. She thought about Doris's airy kisses and Gran scoffing. She thought about Doris whispering to Jennifer-the-Cloth-Doll.

'Oh,' she said to the empty room and did a little drum roll on the table with her pencils. She wrote: *J is for Jennifer-the-Cloth-Doll who knows all Doris's secrets.*

Perry looked at the sentence for a while, then took her eraser, rubbed out *Doris* and wrote *Molly* instead, because it was an ACB for Gran after all.

q e d

That Saturday Perry's father wanted to walk with Perry to Santa Lucia. It was the first time ever. Usually he was in a hurry, he had things to do, places to go, people to see, he needed to drive everywhere, he said, though of course he did rue and regret it. Cars were a curse, he said, but what could you do? What could you do?

'Not drive,' said Perry.

'It's the modern world, my little nymph,' said her father. 'So much to do, so little time. QED: car a necessary evil.'

'Two cars,' said Perry. There was one each for Perry's mother and father.

But this Saturday morning something had come

over him, said her father, he felt like stretching his
legs. It was most strange.

'Perhaps you're sick,' said Perry's mother.

'Hardy ha,' said her father. 'It's a nice winter's
morning, I'm taking a leaf out of Perry's book . . .'

'What book?' said Perry. She stood in her parents'
bedroom, ready and waiting with her backpack and
ACB materials. She wore her new hat.

'Not an actual book, it's a figure of speech—'

'What's a figure of speech?'

'It's a way of saying something . . . a different way of saying something. It's a—'

Perry's father waved his hands. '—it's a,' he made a face at her mother. 'What *is* it, exactly?'

'I'm a psychologist,' said Perry's mother. She was putting in her contact lenses. She grimaced and rolled her eyes and blinked rapidly. She looked as though she'd eaten something very bitter.

'I'm a psychologist with a conference in one week!' She rifled hurriedly through the papers in her satchel.

'What is QED, then?' Perry asked.

'Quod erat demonstrandum,' said Perry's father, promptly.

Conversations at home were *J is for Jolly Odd*, too, thought Perry. She stretched her mouth and rolled

her eyes and blinked rapidly at her father.

'Enough of that,' said her father.

'I'm a Figure of No Speech,' said Perry and was most pleased when her parents burst out laughing.

always zebras

Perry's father wanted to walk on the left side of the river. It was quicker, he said.

'But we're not in a hurry, remember,' said Perry. 'It's much better on the other side. You can walk through the fern reserve. It's dark and *worrying*.' She groaned it happily. That was what Claude did.

'I've got enough worries,' said her father.

'You can have a drink at the little fountain. And you can walk over the wooden bridge. It makes a cheerful sound.'

'Does it just,' said her father.

'You have to watch out for dog poo. And you have to pick up any rubbish and put it in the bin at the park.'

'*Have* to?'

'It's good for the *planet*.'

'Aha!'

'If it was still summer you'd have to look for half asleep or deceased bumblebees.'

'You've got it all sorted, I see,' said her father. He had his eyes on the ground, watching for dog poo.

'And while you're walking you could think of some zeds. Z is the hardest.'

'Zebra.'

'It's *always* zebras in ABCs,' said Perry, witheringly. 'This one's about Gran and Santa Lucia.

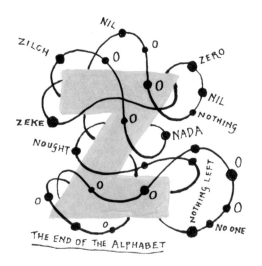

'And a bit about me,' she added.

'Sorry then,' said her father, though he didn't sound it.

'Try again,' said Perry.

'Zoo,' said her father, after twenty steps.

'Try *harder*,' said Perry.

'Zip,' said her father, after thirty-four steps. 'There must be plenty of zippers at Santa Lucia.'

There were, and most of the residents had trouble with them. They got their undies stuck in the teeth of the zip, or they left the zips undone accidentally. Perry had often helped Gran and Doris and Beverley with their zips. Loto said she was a natural. But zips were somehow not very interesting.

'Keep trying,' said Perry.

They entered the fern reserve and emerged before her father spoke again.

'*Zither*,' he said, 'but don't suppose there's any at Santa Lucia. *Zinc*, people take it for colds, could be some there.

'*Zephyr*.' He was ticking them off on his fingers. '*Zodiac. Zigzag*. What do you think of that?'

'Better,' said Perry, after a moment. 'You're improving.

'Slowly,' she said.

steep peak

That night Perry turned to the Z page and drew a large oval. It filled the entire page. She shaded it with the mint green pencil and decorated the edges with stars (for *zodiac*) and lightning bolts (for *zigzag*) and flowers with orange petals (for *zinnia*, which was a flower, but did *not* grow in Kaka garden). She drew zebras in the four corners of the page and some zippers, open and shut. She drew a stern face (for *Zeus* who was a Greek god, according to Bernard, but also not anywhere at Santa Lucia) and a mountain with a steep peak (for *zenith*) and an old stone building (for *Zagreb*, which was a lovely city in Croatia, said Eric, who had been there in his Youth).

In the middle of the large oval she wrote: *Z is for Zero because there is nothing suitable for Z in this ACB*.

measuring the marigold

On Sunday Perry woke with a sore throat. They couldn't go for brunch and she couldn't visit Gran in case she passed on germs. It wouldn't be responsible, said her mother.

'But I won't open my mouth,' said Perry. 'Promise. I'll just do the ACB, I'll keep my head down, I won't breathe on anyone, I won't talk at all. *Promise*. There's only a week to *go* and we still have three letters.'

No, no, no, said her mother, and her father agreed. There would still be time, they said, and who was she kidding about keeping her mouth shut?

She could keep her mouth closed all day if she wanted, Perry said, she'd just show them. But after twenty minutes her teeth were sore from clenching and she needed a warm drink because her throat was dry and aching. Her parents were quite kind about it.

So she lay in bed for a while reading *Bumblebee:*

fortunate friend by Gordon T. Walker. Nina had bought it for her.

Then she lay on the floor of the family room and drew Figures of Speech all in a row: Karl, Peter Pascoe, Doris and Gran. Words fell out of the Figures' mouths: Dutch words, cricket words, the words of songs and *that'll be the Frosty Friday* . . .

She drew two Figures of No Speech: Beverley with her mouth open and no words coming, and Perry herself with her mouth clamped shut and her cheeks puffed out, ready to explode.

On Monday morning Perry had a temperature and a cough and her mother said she must stay in bed.

'I hate bed,' Perry croaked. She was hot *and* cold and clammy and dizzy and her head ached and her eyes were sore and when she swallowed it was as if there were staples in her throat.

'I really am sorry,' said her mother. 'But bed is the best place.' She kissed Perry distractedly. Her head was filled with conference organizing.

Nina made lemon drinks and chicken broth. She put cool cloths on Perry's forehead and spooned Pamol into her mouth. She drew the curtains to keep out the light. Claude stood in the doorway and sang *Inch Worm, Inch Worm, Measu-RING the Mari-GOLD.* Perry tried to think about U and Y and X, but her head throbbed and her legs were restless and her feet itched and the bed sheet kept creasing.

On Tuesday there were small red spots all over Perry's face and body.

'It can't be measles,' said her mother. 'You've been inoculated.' She stared at Perry as if she were a difficult puzzle.

'It's probably a new strain of measles,' said Perry's father, darkly. 'Something resistant. That's happening all the time now.'

But Nina said it would be just a virus, and things would be better now the rash had appeared. Then your temperature went down. You began to feel better.

'I *am* better,' said Perry, though actually she felt more tired than a half asleep bumblebee. 'I can go and see Gran,' she said with great heartiness, but that made her cough.

There would be no seeing Gran, said both her mother and Nina, until the rash had *dis*appeared. Then she would no longer be contagious.

'BUT THEN IT WILL BE SCHOOL!' Perry yelled. 'AND I NEED A YOOOOOOOO . . .' But yelling made her cough worse, and the coughing made her cry and the crying blocked up her nose.

'Poor Perry,' said her mother, and stroked her spotty forehead. 'What about U for *unwell*? Or for *upset*?'

'Or for UGLY,' sobbed Perry, when she saw her face in the mirror. It was quite repulsive.

But that evening Perry's father arrived home with a Get Well present. It was wrapped in shiny yellow paper and was as heavy as a brick.

'I heard you were *unhappy*,' he said. 'This might be *useful*.'

It was a dictionary.

'There may not be *unicorns* or *ukuleles* at Santa Lucia, but there might be . . . let's see . . .' Her father turned the pages quickly . . . '*Umbrellas*?' he said, hopefully.

'There *are* umbrellas,' croaked Perry, sitting up in bed. 'They're in the big urn by the front door. They take them on their outings if it's raining. Except first they have to go and check in Mary Foley's room, because she always hides the umbrellas under her bed so people have to go and collect them and put them back in the urn—

'*URN!*' shrieked Perry.

everyone and everything

On Wednesday morning Perry felt a little better, and her spots were no longer hot. She sat in bed and slowly turned the pages of the ACB. She thought about the cover. What should she draw? She thought about the title. Mrs. Warren said titles were important. Perry wrote some down and considered them.

The A to Z of Santa Lucia (and Me).
The A to Z of Everyone and Everything at Santa Lucia (and Me).
The A to Z of Gran (and Me).
The Anarchic Alphabet.
The Crazy Abecedary.
She smiled at the rhyme.

ancient, cracked

That afternoon Perry and Claude studied the bumblebee collection with a magnifying glass. All the bees had curled up now. They were like sleeping babies, twenty-two all together in a nursery, each wrapped in fading striped fur. Their papery wings looked like ancient, cracked windows.

dream

On Thursday morning Perry woke smiling.

'Now there's only one letter left,' she told her mother.

'Good.' Her mother was shaking the thermometer. 'Which one?'

'Y,' said Perry.

'What did you find for X? Was it in the dictionary?'

'No,' said Perry. She sucked on the thermometer until it pinged.

'It was in my dream.'

losing heart

In the afternoon Perry lay on the floor in the family room once more and called out Y words from her new dictionary.

'*Yak. Yam. Yarn. Yawn.*'

'Yawn's good,' said Nina.

There was quite a bit of yawning at Santa Lucia, it was true. On sunny afternoons there were actually great choruses of yawning in the community room. Sometimes Peter Pascoe or Beverley or little Olga fell suddenly asleep, their heads dropped back, their mouths fell open, snorts and snuffles and snores were heard.

Gran never slept of course. She was too busy, searching for pupils, chasing down Audrey, tidying out other people's drawers and organizing things in Sets.

'*Yodel. Yogurt. Yoke. Yolk.*'

'*Egg* yolks. They have eggs there,' said Nina.

They had scrambled eggs; Perry had seen them at Santa Lucia supper. The eggs were pale and wettish and they slid unappealingly around the plate. Gran sometimes offered her a spoonful, but Perry said no thank you, very politely.

'They have eggs,' she said to Nina. 'But everyone has eggs. Yolks are everywhere.'

'*Yodel, yodel,*' Claude sang, breathlessly. He was doing junior press-ups, rather crookedly, and puffing a great deal. His friend James had taught him at kindergarten.

'*Yellow?*' Nina suggested. She held up a yellow tea towel, raised her eyebrows.

'Yellow is everywhere,' said Perry. She was losing heart with Y.

'Yel*low*, yel*low*,' sang Claude. 'Measu-RING the Mari-GOLD.'

smooth white cheek

By Friday morning Perry's spots had almost gone.

'Can I see Gran tomorrow?' she asked. 'I feel a *hundred* percent better.' This was almost a hundred percent true.

'Probably,' said her mother. She was packing an overnight bag for the conference; she was staying for two nights. 'Very probably. Your father can decide.'

She sprayed perfume under her jaw. 'How do I look?'

Perry studied her mother. She was wearing a suit and shoes with high heels. Her hair was pulled up on top of her head. She had new crimson earrings and lipstick to match. She held her overnight bag tight by her side.

'Like a psychologist,' said Perry.

'Very funny,' said her mother.

'An *organized* psychologist.'

'That'll have to do,' said her mother. 'Wish me luck.'

'Good luck,' said Perry. She kissed her mother on her smooth white cheek.

'An organized psychologist who smells nice,' said Perry.

fat lot of good

Nina and Claude came again on Saturday because Perry's father had to work, too. He had meetings with people. People from Japan, he said. They were only coming for the weekend. Damn nuisance, he said. Couldn't be helped, he said.

'I'll say hello to Gran from you,' said Perry.

She couldn't wait to see Gran. It had been a whole week.

'She doesn't really know who I am,' said her father, crossly.

'She doesn't really know who anyone is,' said Perry. 'But she knows lots of other things.'

'Like what?'

'Songs and poems and riddles and things. Sayings and things.'

'Fat lot of good that is,' said her father.

'That's what Gran says!' said Perry, amazed.

'She does not,' said her father.

'She *does*,' said Perry. 'When anyone gives her her pills she always says, "Fat lot of good this'll do!"'

'Huh,' said her father. He was silent, his brow furrowed.

'Huh,' he said again.

'Anyway,' he said, 'I'd better go. Time waits for no man.'

Perry smiled to herself.

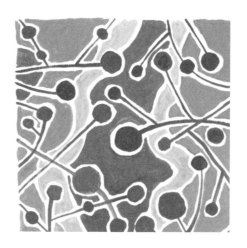

fortunate friend

It was very nice walking around the river after a week inside the house being hot and itchy and weary and fractious. Everything looked new, better. The grass was longer. It was silky and lush. The willows seemed more graceful, the fern reserve darker and wetter and so much more worrying. Claude held Perry's hand and sang *Inch Worm*.

'Guess what I found out about bumblebees,' Perry said.

They still watched out for the bee bodies even though they knew it was too cold and all the bees had disappeared.

'They only live for four weeks,' said Perry, before Nina could answer.

'Brief but beautiful,' said Nina.

'They do all their work in four weeks,' said Perry. 'It was in *Bumblebee: fortunate friend* by Gordon T. Walker.'

'Making honey?' said Nina.

'They don't make much honey,' said Perry. 'They're for pollinating. It's most important.'

After a while she said, 'Four weeks isn't long for something important.'

'Spose that's all the time they need,' said Nina.

'Bumble*bee*, Bumble*bee*,' sang Claude. 'Measu-RING the Mari-GOLD.'

'Four weeks is hardly anything,' said Perry.

'Any*thing*, any*thing*,' sang Claude. He swung Perry's arm in slow arcs, back and forth, back and forth, marking the beat. 'Measu-RING the Mari-GOLD.'

'Probably the bees don't mind,' said Nina. 'They must be used to it.'

yellows blues purples oranges

There was sad news at Santa Lucia. Little Olga had passed away on Wednesday night.

'Pasta Way?' said Claude, as he and Nina waved good-bye. 'What's Pasta Way?'

'Deceased,' said Perry. 'Like the bees.'

'She started going downhill on Sunday,' said Stephen. 'But the family had time to come. They were all here.'

'But she wasn't sick,' said Perry. 'What happened?'

'She was just a tired little body,' said Stephen. 'Ninety-seven years. That's pretty old.'

Stephen was preparing the medication trolley. He counted pills into tiny paper cups and stuck nametag stickers on the rims. He ticked off the names on a list. He lined the pill cups up in neat rows. He was very methodical.

'So most of the staff are at Olga's funeral,' said Stephen. 'I'm holding the fort. Just as well you came, you can give me a hand.'

'I wish I could've gone,' said Perry. She had never been to a funeral.

'I like a good funeral,' said Stephen. 'I like a good funeral hymn.'

'What *is* a hymn?' said Perry. 'Charles Wesley wrote six thousand of them. He must of liked them a lot, too.'

Stephen gave her a look.

'Just something I know,' said Perry.

'It's a religious song,' said Stephen.

'Do you know any?' said Perry.

'Quite a few,' said Stephen. 'Not six thousand.'

'Guess what?' said Perry.

'Hmmmm?' said Stephen. He was pouring something syrupy from a bottle.

'Bumblebees only live for four weeks,' said Perry.

She studied the pills in the paper cups. They were very colorful, bright pinks and yellows, blues and purples and oranges. She read the nametags on the paper cups, moving her lips to the syllables: Mary Foley, Peter Pascoe, Karl van Zyl, Dorothy Horrocks, Beverley Dabrowski, Eleanor Anderson, Uta Sander. No Doris, no little Olga.

'Really?' said Stephen. 'They get a lot done in four weeks.'

'Mostly pollinating,' said Perry. She was trying to remember Olga's last name.

'Olga had a lot of children,' said Perry.

'Nine,' said Stephen. 'Most of them were here. And grandchildren and great-grandchildren. There was quite a crowd round her bed.'

Blackett. Perry remembered the name from Olga's bedroom door. Olga Blackett.

Stephen smiled. 'Your Gran was there too sometimes. No show without your Gran.'

'Did she brush Olga's hair?' Gran liked to brush people's hair, especially Beverley's and Olga's because theirs was the longest.

'No. She was busy tidying,' said Stephen. He grinned at Perry. 'She tidied all Olga's drawers, she arranged everything in Sets. And she dusted. No one seemed to mind. You coming?'

'I'll push the trolley,' Perry said.

Stephen held open the double doors.

'At least we're not mayflies,' he said, following Perry through the door. 'They only live for a day.'

The trolley rattled very pleasingly along the corridor.

'On the other hand,' Stephen said, 'some clams live for more than two hundred years. But, really, who wants to hang round all that time in cold water?'

no voice will tell

Gran was in the peacock cushion room. She was plumping the cushions and dusting the arms of the sofa with a towel.

'Hello Gran,' said Perry.

'Well, well,' said Gran, standing up straight as a pole. 'Look what the wind blew in.'

'I've had a virus,' said Perry. 'But I'm not contagious any more.'

She hugged Gran's waist quickly. 'I missed you, Gran!'

'And I'm Mickey Mouse,' said Gran. She dusted Perry's neck with the towel.

Perry knelt down at the coffee table. She opened up the ACB and took out her crayons and pencils.

'This is a turn-up for the books,' said Gran. 'Someone's done some homework.' She stuffed the towel duster down the front of her jersey. It wasn't her jersey, Perry knew, it was too big. It was like a great baggy dress.

'I *have* done some homework,' said Perry. 'I've done so much there's only one letter to go.'

'Pleased to hear it,' said Gran. She knelt unsteadily beside Perry and banged the table forward.

'Whoops!' said Perry, grabbing Gran's arm. Bernard always said *Whoops!* whenever anyone crashed or bumped or fell over.

'What have you got for me?' said Gran, brightly. There was a long scabby scratch on her jaw.

'What happened, Gran?' said Perry. She touched the scratch gently.

'Don't worry about that,' said Gran, batting her hand away. 'How's that writing shaping up?'

Perry slowly turned the pages of the ACB and Gran peered intently. She couldn't really see properly, Perry knew. Her glasses had been missing for a while. She'd thrown them over the vine-covered fence or in the rubbish bin one too many times and now no one could find them. They were waiting for new ones from the optician.

'Not bad,' said Gran. 'Not bad at all.

'You'll do,' she said, squinting at Perry. Perry leaned into her a little. She smelled of peppermints.

'There's just Y now,' said Perry.

'Why?' said Gran. 'Why indeed?'

'Y,' said Perry.

'Why oh why oh why?' said Gran.

She stood creakily and sat on the sofa. The duster stuck out of her chest beneath the big jersey, like a hidden baby.

'Why is a raven like a writing desk?' said Gran.

'Why is a raven like a *writing desk*?' Perry repeated. 'I don't know. Are they the same color?'

'There's no answer,' said Gran.

'Y is for . . . ?' Perry suggested.

'Why, why, why, why, why, why, why?' said Gran. It was a little song, a little groaning song, trailing away.

'Y . . . ?' said Perry again, drawing out the sound. But Gran was staring off, her mouth a little open.

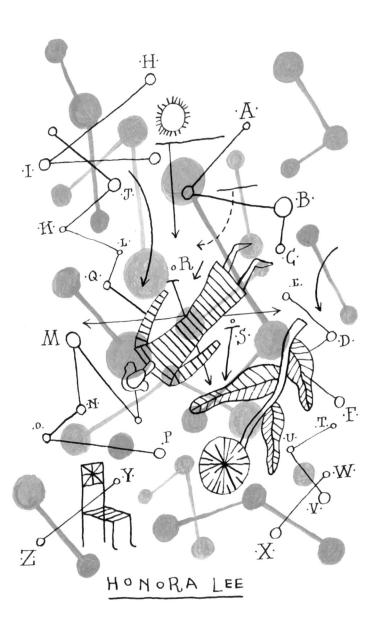

HONORA LEE

'*Why did I laugh tonight?*' said Gran. '*No voice will tell . . .*'
She laid her head back on the sofa, as if she were
suddenly very tired.

Perry got up and sat on the sofa beside her. She
watched Gran's face closely. A small droplet seeped
from Gran's eye and rested in the ridges of wrinkles.

'Are you all right, Gran?' said Perry. She found
Gran's hand, cool and rough, and massaged it gently
as she had seen Paula and Loto and Barbara do.

Gran said nothing, her humpy chest went up
and down, up and down, as if she were short of
breath, as if she had been climbing steps.

Perry leaned into Gran and blew gently on her
cheek. 'Gran,' she said, 'Gran? Who am I?'

Gran turned, brushing her cheek irritably.
'What?' she said.

Not *What*, thought Perry. *I beg your pardon.*

'Who am I?' said Perry again.

'Well,' said Gran, tartly, 'if you don't know *I* can't
help you.'

'Who *am* I?' insisted Perry, staring into Gran's
watery eyes.

'Ha,' said Gran. 'Don't think you can fool me!'

'You're your*self*!' she said, very firmly. She laid
her head back on the sofa.

Perry laid her head back on the sofa, too, and
they were both still, just for a moment.

very good indeed

On the first Thursday of the new term, Perry took the completed ACB to Santa Lucia to show everyone.

She had stayed up very late on Sunday finishing the cover and title. She lay on the floor drawing while her mother and father talked about Japanese visitors and psychologists.

On Monday she had handed in the ACB to Mrs. Warren. On Wednesday Mrs. Warren had handed it back to her.

'Most original, Perry,' said Mrs. Warren, with a laugh. She had a grinding little laugh, like a kookaburra.

'Unique,' laughed Mrs. Warren.

'Very inventive,' she said. 'I can honestly say I've never seen anything like it. A+ for effort! Shall we leave it on the Display Table so the rest of the class can see it?'

'No thank you,' said Perry, most politely. 'I have to show it somewhere else.'

Nina had made a cake to celebrate the ACB. 'C for chocolate,' she said, holding up the cake. The dark icing shone.

'E for enormous,' said Perry.

'Choco-LATE, choco-LATE,' sang Claude.

At Santa Lucia they passed the ACB around the community room and the office and the kitchen.

Some of the residents read it slowly, some just held it and stared at the cover.

'*P is for Peter Pascoe*,' crowed Peter Pascoe. 'Look at that!' He didn't want to let the ACB go.

'*P is for Peter Pascoe*! Peter Pascoe, ha!' He stared and stared at the P page.

'Peter Pascoe for Prime Minister!' shouted Melvyn Broome and banged his walking stick up and down.

Audrey laughed so much she had a small wheezing attack.

'Magnificent,' said Loto, as she leafed through the book. 'This is a work of art.'

Paula enveloped Perry in a hug. She smelled of soap and the medicine room and old people. 'What a wonderful granddaughter,' she said, squeezing.

'Good title,' said Bernard.

'Do you like the title, Gran?' Perry asked. Gran was sitting briefly, eating a second piece of chocolate cake. She ate the icing first. Perry wished that Doris were there, too.

Bernard showed the cover to Gran.

'*ACB with Honora Lee*,' said Gran through the cake crumbs. 'Somebody doesn't know their ABC properly.'

'It's artistic license,' said Bernard.

'My big toe it is,' said Gran.

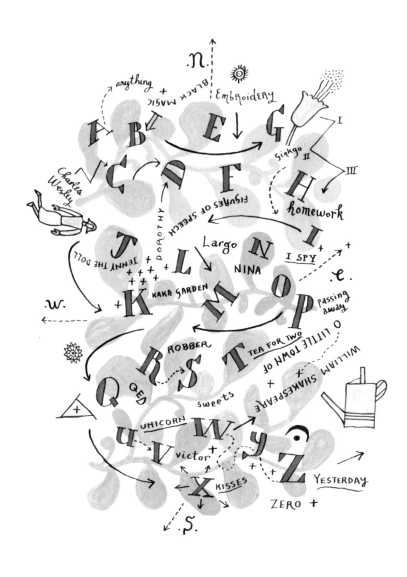

'*Honora Lee*,' said Perry. 'It's you, Gran.'

'Of course it is,' said Gran. 'I should think so, too.'

'I still don't know what X is,' said Eric. He was scooping the last of the icing from the plate with his finger. 'Is it xylophone?'

'No,' said Perry, 'and it's not x-ray, either.'

'It's a good one,' said Paula.

'I dreamt it,' said Perry. 'What's X for, Gran?'

'Excellence,' said Gran. She turned the pages of the book. 'T, U, V, W, X—'

'There,' said Perry, stopping Gran on the X page. She pointed to the line.

'X is for,' Gran read, and stopped. She scowled at the page. Perry had drawn red lips, big and small, all over the X page.

'Huh,' said Gran, '*kisses*.'

'Oh yes, very good,' said Eric. He had a chocolate smear on his upper lip. 'Very good indeed.'

'*Yes*,' said Perry. 'C'mon Gran.' She put her hands on Gran's bony cheeks. 'X is for kisses.' She puckered her lips like Doris.

'If you *insist*,' said Gran, screwing up her face. She closed her eyes and pushed her lips into a stiff little pucker.

Perry kissed Gran gently.

'B is for bristly,' she said.

ANTA LUCIA

later

all is calm, all is bright

Perry and Nina and Claude had a funeral for the bumblebees. They made a funeral procession around the river, over the pedestrian crossing, through the fern reserve and across the little wooden bridge into the loop where there was a wide flat bank.

Claude walked in front carrying the bees in a yogurt container. Perry and Nina walked behind with flowers, snowdrops and winter sweet and Solomon's seal.

'Do you know any hymns?' Perry asked Nina.

'I know Christmas Carols,' said Nina.

'Are they hymns?'

'Not exactly,' said Nina.

'We could sing *Silent Night*,' said Perry. 'All is calm, all is bright.'

Perry and Claude walked as close to the river-bank as possible and scattered the bees on the water. It had been raining for the last few days so the river was high and running fast. The bees were swept away immediately, under the wooden bridge and out of sight.

They sang *Silent Night*, one verse, very softly.

Claude sang *Inch Worm*.

Perry imagined the bumblebees, racing down the river, under all the bridges, past ducks and

riverweed and the tips of willows, dodging leaves
and bread crusts.

'Where are they going?' asked Claude.

'To the sea,' said Perry.

'The sea, the sea,' said Claude, taking her hand.

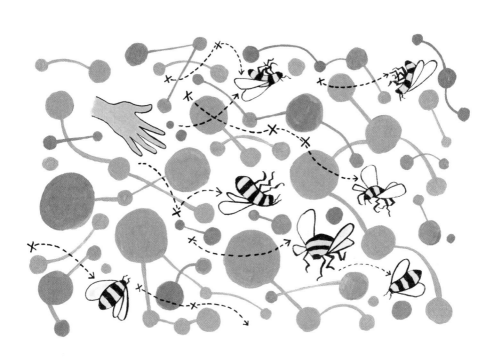

Also by Kate De Goldi

Clubs: A Lolly Leopold Story
Uncle Jack
Billy: A Lolly Leopold Story
The Ten PM Question

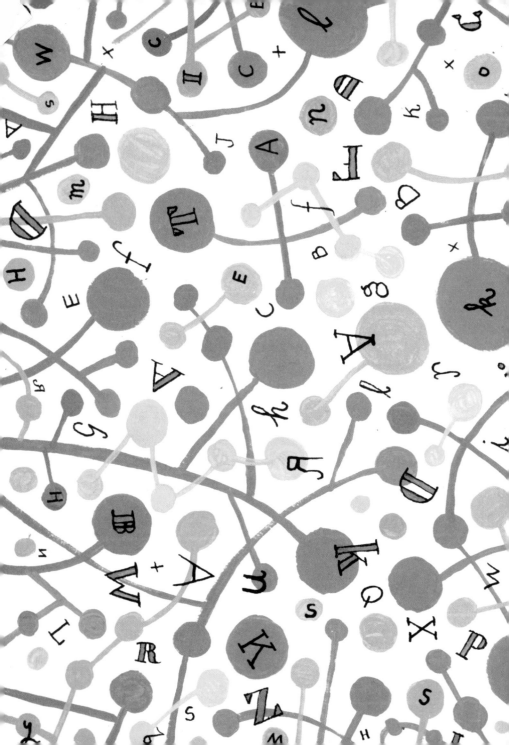